DAN JAMES

HELIUM DREAM

and the Lost Heart

For all children, young and old, far and wide.

AMETHYST BOOKS LIMITED
PO Box 231, Uxbridge, Middlesex

Only the familiar whine of the milkfloat clinking down the street, interrupted the otherwise silent, early hours. Carly was sitting in her pyjamas on the living room floor, concentrating on her latest jigsaw puzzle. Dad was busily searching through the bathroom cabinet.

"Who's had my razor?"

"Carly, have you touched it?" shouted Dad, "What have I told you about playing with razors?"

At five years, Carly was neither old enough to shave, nor tall enough to reach the razor, even if she could have grown a beard! Nevertheless, she happened to be the nearest target for Dad's moans.

Almost in tears, she gazed out of the window and looked dreamily at the sky. The sun began to filter through the high morning clouds, and one by one, the street lamps flickered off to announce daybreak.

TILLYER

"Ah! Here it is," said Dad triumphantly, and began to shave. The radio played quietly to itself in the kitchen. Carly was just about to fit the last piece of her jigsaw, when she was distracted by Dad making loud squeaking noises, as he frantically rubbed the mirror with his forearm.

"What's wrong with this useless mirror?" He fumed, "First the missing razor, now the missing reflection – I think I must be going blind!"

"Carly, go and ask Mum for a cloth please, so that I can clean this mirror," ordered Dad.

As Carly reached the stairs, Mum was coming down, with bright pink lipstick smeared all over her chin. Carly erupted into a fit of giggles as Mum swept past her, heading for the bathroom.

"What on *earth* is going on?," said Dad, with a puzzled look on his frothy half-shaven face, "have you seen what's happened to this mirror?"

"It's not only the mirrors you know," added Mum, "look at the windows too, *all* the reflections are missing."

In sheer confusion, Mum and Dad dashed to the front door and threw it open, to expose a street buzzing with neighbours pointing and chattering to each other, holding mirrors and once-reflective objects of all shapes and sizes. Carly bounced on to the sofa, lifted the net curtain over her head and gazed out, enthralled by all this excitement.

All things considered, the Townfolk returned to routine extremely peacefully, almost forgetting about the odd happening, except for the dull reminders all around them. Saturday lunch-time shopping was always busy, so Mum, Dad, and Carly, rushed from shop to shop, hoping to escape before the afternoon queues built up. Heading back to the car, Carly led Dad over to a street vendor selling metallic helium-filled balloons, who looked as though he was just about to float away.

"That's one-fifty please mate," said the man as he pulled a heart shaped balloon from the bunch, "sorry Guv', but they ain't very shiny. Still, I s'pose you know that already?"

Dad grunted, and fumbling with his loose change to find the right money, he looked up at the rain filled sky.

TILLYER 88.

"UGH!" Not rain *again*," he groaned, "We'd better get back to the car."

"Come on Carly get a move on!" agreed Mum as they hurried along the pavement.

Carly couldn't care less about the rain, now that she had her new balloon to play with. (She'd pestered Dad every weekend to buy her another one after her best friend popped the last one.) On the way home in the car, she periodically tugged at the string, fascinated at how the balloon always floated upwards and stuck to the roof.

"Why isn't it shiny like the last balloon Daddy?"

In the front of the car Mum and Dad glanced at each other, both wishing Carly hadn't asked that question. In the bustle of shopping they had almost forgotten about the strange event earlier that day. Soon they were home, and Carly went straight into the back garden to play with her new balloon.

"Carly, make sure you tie it to your wrist so that you don't lose it," said Mum as she closed the car door that Carly had left wide open. With her new balloon trailing behind, she rode her bike round and round the back garden. Suddenly, a distant-sounding voice called out her name.

AILY NEWS
TS HAPPENED
REFLECTIONS!
ritai
Tidy

"Carly! Quickly. I must talk to you."

Carly jumped off her bike in surprise and looked all around, but saw no-one. "Not over there – Here Carly. I'm in the balloon! Can't you see me?"

Carly pulled the balloon down to her face, and as she looked hard into the dull surface, she could just distinguish a tiny figure smiling back at her.

"I can see you!" said Carly excitedly, "But who are you?"

"I'm your reflection! – Well, I'm supposed to be your reflection, but as you can see things aren't going too well here at the moment."

"What do you mean, *there?*" asked Carly, quite confused.

"This is the land of reflections of course! Now listen carefully; I need your help to bring all the reflections back, so trust me and do EXACTLY as I say. Put your hand against the balloon until it touches mine."

Carly nervously did as she was asked, but the moment she touched the balloon, her hand mysteriously passed right in to the surface.

TILLYER/88

She jumped as a tiny hand grasped hers, and in an instant everything around her shattered in to countless fragments, as she was pulled from the ground with great force. Rolling through space she twisted and turned, and gathering speed she hurtled towards a distant point of light.

Moments later, she found herself standing on a beautifully lush, grassy-green hillside, holding hands with her own reflection.

"Are you OK Carly?," said the blurred image tugging at her hand.

"I . . . I . . . think so," said Carly a little shakily.

"Hello, I'm your reflection. Now don't speak, just listen very carefully; you must hold my hand very tightly and not let go, or else you'll return to your world and won't ever be able to come here again."

Carly looked a little concerned, "Won't Mum and Dad worry if they can't find me?"

"They won't be looking for you, because while your here time in the real world stands still, so you'll be back at the time you left. Oh . . . there is one thing I have to tell you . . .

when the two Suns meet in the sky, you must return to your world or you'll never be able to leave."

Carly looked confused, "How do you know ALL that?" she asked inquisitively.

"The Mirror Man told me so, and he knows just about EVERYTHING!" said her reflection confidently.

"Who's the Mirror Man?" asked Carly.

"He's the man who makes the mirror images and reflections of everything in the entire universe, but at the moment he's stuck on a reflection he just cannot sort out. When he isn't happy, all your mirrors and shiny things cease to reflect. I'm afraid at the moment he's pretty miserable, so that's why you're here . . . do you see?"

"Oh yes," nodded Carly, not really seeing at all, "but why can't *you* help him?" Her reflection pondered for a moment.

"Well . . . it's like this. I'm a reflection, and reflections aren't real . . . right?"

"Right," answered Carly positively.

"And you *are* real . . . right?"

"Right."
"So if I'm not real, I can't possibly solve a *real* problem . . . right?"
"Er . . . RIGHT!" said Carly, completely satisfied with a very unsatisfactory explanation.
"The Mirror Man lives in a little rose-covered cottage over that hill," pointed Carly's reflection, "so we'll have to hurry, because the Suns are getting close – come on!"
With that Carly was half dragged by her reflection, down one hill and over the next until, out of breath, they reached the Mirror Man's cottage. The door was slightly ajar, and Carly's reflection peered through the gap.
"YOO HOO! . . . HELLO Mr Mirror Man, are you in there?"
She prodded the old oak door and slowly it creaked open. In the corner of a room filled with antiques and bric-a-brac, was a huge wooden rocking chair, and there sat a wrinkled old man, wearing a crumpled grey suit. Rocking gently back and forth, he raised his eyes from a book on his lap, and peered over the rim of his half-glasses.
"Shouldn't you be reflecting Carly young lady?" he said sternly.

TILLYER 89

"Er . . . actually Mr Mirror Man sir, she's here!" and she yanked Carly in to view.

"Well . . . well . . . well," said the Mirror Man, "the *real* Carly! Come in child, and tell me why you've come to this place?"

"I've been brought here to help you restore our reflections." said Carly boldly. She looked at her reflection and shrugged her shoulders, not really knowing what to do or say next. The Mirror Man ceased rocking, and laying his book aside, he leaned forward in his chair.

"So young lady, what makes you think *you* can solve my problem?"

Carly took a deep breath and stepped closer to the Mirror Man.

"I don't know sir," she said politely, "but please can I try? We want our reflections back, because without them my Dad can't shave properly, and my Mum can't put on her make-up." She paused for thought, "Do you know how dangerous it is to drive cars and lorries without mirrors? Dentists need mirrors to see around teeth properly . . . and what about those bendy mirrors you see in fairgrounds? Think of the fun they give people! We all need your reflections very much."

TILLYER 89

The Mirror Man leaned back, pointing at all the objects around his room.

"Let me tell you something Carly; I've worked in this room making reflections of all and sundry for umpteen billion years since time began, and I suddenly realised the other day, that not once has anyone bothered to come here and say thank you . . . not ONCE! I really wish I'd taken an easier job like 'shadow making', for all the thanks I get here! It's become so difficult lately, I can't even make a simple reflection of this funny little thing I was given this morning – I'll show you."

As he spoke, he pulled out from under his chair the strangest looking object Carly had ever seen. (In fact, it was an impossible shaped object.)

"Not so many centuries ago, I would've had a reflection of this knocked out in a flash, but this one has me tied up in knots. I've tried this way and that, hour after hour, but I just cannot fathom it out!" he said scratching his head.

Carly wanted to look closer at this shape, but as she reached out her hand to take it from the Mirror Man, a strange thing happened – her hand passed clean through it. Stranger still, she couldn't touch it, or even feel it!

The Mirror Man leapt from his chair.

"AH – HA!" he yelled excitedly. "So THAT's it . . . silly me, it's not real at all!"

Carly's reflection butted in, "And if it isn't real, it can't have a reflection . . . right?"

The Mirror Man walked over to a cabinet, and placing the object inside, he locked the door and hid the small key high on a shelf.

"THAT can stay in there for good!" he said, and smiled for the first time that day. As he did so, his old crumpled grey suit began to glint and shimmer with colour. So much so that Carly jumped back in astonishment! The Mirror Man chuckled to himself and gently patted Carly on the head.

"Thank you Carly . . . very much. Now I can at last get on with my work. Honestly, how could I have forgotten that?" He broke into infectious laughter and his brilliantly shiny mirror-like suit reflected all that was around him.

"Of course . . . of course!" he muttered to himself as he bounded into the garden, squinting in the bright sunlight. The flowers, fields and sky all mirrored in the surface of his dazzling attire.

As he danced around and around, Carly stood by the cottage door, spellbound by the glittering spectacle she witnessed before her.

"Come on Carly, we must go now," said her reflection as she tugged on her hand once more. "Look how close the Suns are!" The Mirror Man saw them about to leave.

"Wait Carly! I've something to give you." Walking towards her, he slipped his hand into his jacket. From deep in one pocket he pulled out what looked like a piece of tarnished metal, from another, some tiny transparent pebbles. Enclosing them in his large hands, he held out his arms.

"This . . . is for you, to take back to the real world. Its just a little 'Thank-you'." In his hands the objects began to glow, then a whirling kaleidoscope of pulsing multi-coloured light flashed and flickered from between his fingers. When he opened them, there rested the most beautiful, precious, golden jewel, shimmering in the sunlight. Carly gasped in amazement.

"Thanks Mr Mirror Man!", she said, grabbing the jewel and pulling the Mirror Man down by his sleeve to kiss him on the cheek. Waving their goodbyes, Carly and her reflection dashed off up the winding footpath.

TILLYER 89

A few minutes later they were standing atop the very same hill on which Carly had arrived.

"I'm going to have to let go of your hand now Carly," said her reflection. Carly looked down, sadly.

"Can I come back and see you again?" Her reflection paused for a moment.

"No . . . I'm afraid you can't." she said firmly. "But remember, I'll always be with you wherever you go – you'll see me all around you. So just smile at me, and I'll smile back."

Before Carly knew it, the lovely sunny green countryside was once again whorling around her head, everything intermingling with everything else.

Back in her garden, she smiled at her reflection in the gleaming surface of her balloon, and sure enough, her reflection smiled right back. Giant rain-drops splashed onto the path. Suddenly, the string slipped from her wrist.

TILLYER '87

"MY JEWEL! – WHERE'S MY JEWEL!" she cried out, but the jewel was nowhere to be found.

The balloon floated gently upwards, brightening the oppressive late afternoon sky. Just then, the patio door slid open as Mum called excitedly.

"Quickly Carly! Come and see what's happened – all the reflections have come back."

But Carly already knew . . .

TILLYER 89

The Lost Heart is NOT on or near the following: National Trust ground, Private Property, Church ground, Nature reserves, Archaeological sites, Anywhere dangerous, Parks or Gardens, Farm land, Fenced off land.

The Lost Heart is buried about 12″ below the surface, and over half a kilometre from any buildings, private, commercial or otherwise.

The Publisher and Author accept no responsibility for damage or injury resulting from Treasure Hunters activities.

Please act in a responsible manner at all times.

First published 1989 by Amethyst Books Limited, PO Box 231, Uxbridge, Middlesex UB10 9QT

British Library Cataloguing in Publication Data
James, Dan, *1961–*
Helium dream and the lost heart
I. Title
823'.914 [J]
ISBN 1-871785-00-6

Typeset by Rowland Phototypesetting Limited, Bury St Edmunds, Suffolk.
Printed by Arnoldo Mondadori in Italy